A TALE OF TWO DESERTS

Enigmatic Christmas Fables for the Modern Age

A TALE OF TWO DESERTS

Enigmatic Christmas Fables for the Modern Age

by

Paul T Kidd

Cheshire Henbury

First published in 2013 by Cheshire Henbury
ISBN 978-1-901864-16-8

British Library Cataloguing in Publication Data.
A catalogue record for this book is available from the British Library.

Cheshire Henbury
E-mail: books@cheshirehenbury.com

Web site: www.cheshirehenbury.com/ataleoftwodeserts

A TALE OF TWO DESERTS

Enigmatic Christmas Fables for the Modern Age

by

Paul T Kidd

Cheshire Henbury

First published in 2013 by Cheshire Henbury
ISBN 978-1-901864-16-8

British Library Cataloguing in Publication Data.
A catalogue record for this book is available from the British Library.

Cheshire Henbury
E-mail: books@cheshirehenbury.com

Web site: www.cheshirehenbury.com/ataleoftwodeserts

To those who are still able to hear, to see and to understand

Preface

As the sub-title of the book suggests, what you will find here are two very enigmatic tales. After reading them you may ask, what is the point of these stories? What do they mean? This, actually, is the point; the book is an invitation to reflect, to contemplate, to learn and to realise that life is a journey best undertaken with eyes open and with a mind not imprisoned by ideology, in whatever form that may come: religion, capitalism, socialism, atheism, science, engineering, technology … The list seems endless.

To help you to understand these fables, though, I will mention here that the first tale, of the second, makes more sense, and the second tale, of the first, makes more sense. And here I also invite you to reflect upon the narrative that runs across both tales; in some places this narrative is self-evident, and in others less so. Finally, I mention the messages, most important, to be found in these two tales. What can be said of these? The answer is very clear; there are many messages, some obfuscated, some not, and the most profound and clear message, to all the peoples of the world, is to begin to walk a different path, and soon!

Paul T Kidd

July 2013

Contents

"Optimism is a mania for insisting that all is well when all is by no means well"
Voltaire (*Candide*)

"Men's courses will foreshadow certain ends, to which, if persevered in they must lead ..., but if the courses be departed from the ends will change"
Charles Dickens (*A Christmas Carol*)

"Two roads diverged in a wood and I – I took the one less travelled by, and that has made all the difference"
Robert Frost ("The Road Not Taken")

The Desert

There is more here than just words, and more to the words than just mere words; and of deserts, what can be said? Here now find, in words spoken in silence, learning, understanding, and wisdom, for deserts are places where life prospers, even though at times it can seem to some, those perhaps who judge too much based on appearances, that there is no life. Yet there are deserts, not of natural origin you must understand, where life most definitely does not flourish. Yet even in such places, there is still hope for life.

This matter aside, let me proceed to my tale of the desert literal; that place of sun, heat, and features most beautiful. Here life, in that which is nature's creation, can be both cruel and kind, but life does prosper nevertheless. Now see for yourself and learn that here, in this place of hardships, those who dwell in the desert world have little in the way of material comforts, and, in the age to which we now journey, through the power of imagination, even less so than today. Not here will you find any mark of modern civilisation, or extensive knowledge of the universe, that is, ironically, not extensive at all. All this is yet to come, lying thousands of years ahead, in a future that no one could possibly have foreseen, or perhaps they did, but nobody wanted to listen and to take note that there were aspects of this future that should not be.

To what do I refer? This you must discover for yourself, for in the end there are aspects to life, to the universe, and what lies beyond, that cannot be told. All I can do is to help you in this process of discovery, in this most important of life's tasks, and in the pages that follow, you will find the way-markers that I have left for you to help you on this journey. Look out for these signposts, for they are not always as obvious as you might think, they being, I must tell you, part of a language that most people today no longer know, but which, in the time to which I now take you, is part of the natural order of life.

One matter though that I must address before unfolding for you this enigmatic tale of the desert is that of recounting to you what people of the desert in this now distant age did have; most of that which matters!

Here I speak of that which in the contemporary world is all too often sacrificed for the sake of economic growth and personal prosperity, these two goals being very much interlinked. And of that which matters, love is central, not just love for one another, but for the living world that people in this desert still know they are a part of, and which they still respect. There is also service; not what you think of as service, of a person being paid to provide some labour, but of people working together, helping one another, and, in doing so, creating a community that endures. Happiness can also be found, along with the understanding that material possessions are not the source of this happiness, only a way of contributing to life's comforts and helping to make the mechanics of the process of living a little easier. Finally, let us not forget that most intangible of concepts: time! In this desert literal, there is plenty of time, that which you, dear reader, most probably have little that you can call your own. And time to do what? What possibly could these people of a now long-past era have done with their time? This is indeed a question. Of course, it would have been time to think, to reflect, to explore one's inner self, to acquire understandings that can only be attained through reflection and self-questioning, and, of course, time for those people that matter most to us. In short, all activities that consume time, and which represent a good use of that time; all that, in fact, many modern people have little time for. Now I drift to another type of desert, one that is figurative, where life does not flourish.

But back to the desert literal, and in such deserts, as in other wild and untamed places in the world, there is no better place for discovering oneself and learning the humility that comes from understanding our ignorance, out of which comes the true knowledge that we know in fact very little about matters most profound: ourselves and our purpose, and that of the universe in which we dwell. And perhaps the most profound of understandings is that this universe is a work of unfathomable complexity wrought by the hand of unfathomable complexity. The most important knowledge is to know that this is so, and to begin the quest to understand more, and to learn that such a journey can never have a final destination.

Here I feel I must explain, for it is an essential part of my story, and if you will for a moment allow me to digress, I think that you will, deep within you, within the core of your very being, in your soul, recognise an eternal truth, although your mind may rebel against it, which is also at the core of the truth.

What is the true nature of God, this hand of unfathomable complexity? Of course, in the modern era, this is a question not much considered, not even by organised religions, which have now become confined and restricted, as if caged, being also the prisoners of dogma, which to a large extent explains the former. For the most part, organised religions seem largely unable to influence, in a profound and positive way, the mainstream of life, this now being caught up mainly in matters of economic growth, and the delusion that we can know it all. And when religion does have a major impact, it is usually of the most negative kind. Religious beliefs are also now, in the western world, and increasingly so elsewhere, a very private matter, not at all discussed in the public sphere, and certainly not within the worlds of science, technology, economics and business. But there are places where the religions of God are still part of everyday life; yet even where this is the case, in the most fundamental form, there is no distinction from the western world, just different manifestations of the same ignorance that has closed in on fixed opinions, expressed as dogma, unleashing all sorts of evil masquerading as good. I am back once more to the impoverished world of the figurative desert; the one of man's own making. It is forever manifesting itself in my tale!

But you may well say, of God and religion, good riddance! And I can see your point, for we have had enough of the madness that many of those who adhere to the religions of God bring to our world. But I did ask a question, did I not? What is the true nature of God? You think that the people of these religions know the answer to this question? They do not, and far too many of them do not recognise this, hence the lunacy to which I just referred! And the degree to which you care about this question at all, or to which you may be offended by such a statement about religious people's ignorance of God, is a measure of how far you have moved from the true nature of being human.

This is all I will say for now on this question, but be in no doubt that, of this matter, more will be said, for it is a theme most important to a future that should be, and of avoiding one that must not be.

You are perhaps a little mystified. Maybe you do not see the full relevance of my digression. Did I not say that some way-markers are not at all obvious?

Now I return to the desert literal, and to the tale I wish to convey to you, which as I have already stated, and which here I remind you about, is enigmatic.

~

Coldness envelops the desert. You are surprised I think, for this is not that which you were expecting. Perhaps you thought the opposite, and in fact that which would be all too omnipresent would be oppressive heat. Be therefore forewarned that my tale is not that which you might expect. This is also the nature of life. One never knows who will turn up at your door, or who is standing next to you. People are full of surprises! Some are whom they seem, others not so, which does not always mean that they are bad, just perhaps that you never looked closely enough, or that you did not listen to the voice of your soul, which was telling you exactly who was standing next to you; see another way-marker.

But judging by appearances alone is always dangerous. Some folk appear fine, dressed as they are to be part of the world they want to be part of, yet about them hangs the aura of a soul corrupted by power, ambition and greed. Others are the opposite, looking a little shabby and not at all concerned to be part of any world of man's creation, yet about them there is a feeling of love and peace. And in this desert world, such matters are easier to see, for people here are still in tune with themselves and are still able to glimpse, to gain some understanding of, the meaning of the language of unfathomable complexity. But this is often not the case in deserts of man's making, where life does not flourish. This matter is back once again, finding a way to appear in my story, demanding our attention, but for the last time, I promise!

Back to my desert world, my place of mystery and natural splendour, and I will tell you at this point in my tale that the desert is indeed often a place where temperatures rise to sometimes unbearable levels, where all life seeks out any shelter that can be found to escape the remorseless eternal presence that we call the sun; that which has the purpose to give life to our astonishing world, with all its wondrous and boundless diversity.

Even in the desert, though, there are seasons, for nature is always in motion; nothing stays the same. As life moves forward, timeless patterns repeat, year on year. So in this way, time passes. The scorching heat of the summer does eventually end. The vivid colours, hues of red and orange, shifting and changing with the light, creating, for those who watch, impressions of desert life, will shift to a season which has its own but different splendour. To winter the hot season turns, and with the changes comes relief from the overbearing heat; but mark my words, for it is at this time of year that the coldness is at its most dangerous, as this could kill a man just as surely as the heat.

And here now you have the scene. It is winter and, as the night draws in, the cold quickly descends. The sun, now set, leaves behind for many moments, which in their summation amount to almost an hour, a red glow in the western sky, far beyond the horizon, where in fact the sun still shines, for this is the nature of this eternal process; a setting sun is also a shining sun and at the same time also a rising sun. Life, the world, the universe – these are far more complex than they at first appear. This, in this past world we now visit, is part of what is known as an unfathomable complexity shaped by the hand of unfathomable complexity.

High up on a rocky outcrop, overlooking the flat plains far below, sits a solitary figure, a stranger to these desert lands. He has settled here for the night, for evidently it is to be a very special one. Far to the east a new star has burst into life, a portent of some important occurrence, and this man, who sits among the rocks and rough vegetation, knows he should watch and be, in some very small way, a part of this event, although he does not know, and will never know, what it is. We, with hindsight, can however understand, for it is part of a tale that has a resonance with the question not many pages back asked. See, this matter appears once again in my story.

So there he is; a fair-haired, fair-skinned man with blue-grey eyes, in a world of people with darker skins, darker hair and, for the most part, brown eyes. You will learn shortly why this is so and how this came to be.

The Fair-haired One sits on the hard ground, but has made for himself a comfortable resting place for the night. With blankets made from wool, and cushions stuffed with the fleece of mountain sheep, he has a soft place to sit, the means of keeping warm, and is able to rest his back against a boulder and not experience the hardship that such a hard surface would create. Before him also is a bright burning fire, flames dancing, casting orange patterns on his face and all around. A good supply of wood also lies within his reach, for he has no intention of letting the flames die down.

Leaning back against the boulder, blanket draped over his shoulder, one leg stretched out flat on the ground, the other bent with knee raised up to the level of his chin, the Fair-haired One peacefully contemplates the night scene. And what of this stranger? Who is he?

Dear reader, in a few places over the pages that follow, I will begin to enlighten you a small amount about this enigmatic person, for, as you will see later, he is reluctant to speak of some matters relating to himself. But you, to make more sense of this tale, do need to know at least a little of his history. As to why he will not speak about certain aspects of himself, this reflects wisdom, for he knows that it is better to leave people to discover for themselves deeper truths about individuals, the universe, and their connection to it. This, by the way, is another way-marker.

Continuing with my story, we were at the point where the sun had set, which had left a glorious afterglow for all to watch, but time has moved on slightly. The splendour of sunset has now given way to the full darkness of the desert night, and, there being a new moon, stars twinkle clearly in the cold night air, watching down on the Fair-haired One, as though intent on being his patient and uncomplaining companions through the long hours of darkness. And he is not alone, for here in this silence and solitude, he has learned how not to be alone, for there is life everywhere, seen and unseen; life of this world and of others as well, where his soul is still able to reach. Here in this far distant age, you must understand, there are no distractions to make it otherwise, but also he has not allowed himself to become confined by that which others would have him believe; that which is often naught but a mixture of misunderstandings, delusions, lies, deceptions, distortions, and corruptions of the truth, combined with that which is the truth.

He stills his thoughts until they are no more. Then there is just an absence of mental chatter; a flat calm ocean of being, without the turbulence created by emotions and desires. Here is the beginning of that quest for understanding that just goes on, for this is the journey that has no end.

But it was not straightforward reaching this point, for life was determined to test him all the way, which shaped him in ways that for people from a pleasure-seeking, pain-avoiding culture, are truly alien and beyond comprehension. In this way, life, the universe, helped him to become the person that he is. Thus it happened that many difficult challenges of a kind that have the potential to break or make a person continually came at him, sometimes many at once. The outcome from such a maelstrom is everyone's to choose. He could have given up, and many times he nearly did, but at such moments there was always there to help him an invisible hand, and he struggled on, growing stronger and more complete as he did so, but also learning that at each step he was only just beginning his journey.

The choices he made were not straightforward, nor was the path he chose to follow smooth and effortless, and often the trail that seemed most undemanding was not the right one to take. But he learned and slowly started to recognise that those ways that are often most difficult to walk, where the road to follow is less clear, were, in the end, the routes that led to beautiful places. And this is how one's inner self grows and develops, for nothing much ever comes from following the painless way through life. Yet, in the Fair-haired One's past, there was also an experience, very special in character, which changed his life in ways that are difficult to explain and to understand, especially for people caught up in the modern world with its rather peculiar values and beliefs.

One day, now long past, that invisible hand reached out to him, and began to take his soul on a journey, out of this world, to a place that has no name and no form. Led there by that which he recognised and did not fear, he was taken apart, stripped of his worldly interests, destroyed as a man, and very slowly prepared for death, which in the end he was more than willing to embrace. Except he did not die, for, as the tale now being told shows, he was returned to the world of the living, where, with a wounded soul, he slowly began to re-engage with life, but from a very different perspective than that of other men: that of a wounded healer. I will tell you here that this was exactly the aim of the experience to which he was subjected. But why? What was the ultimate purpose of this experience? Why was he taken on this journey? The answer to these questions, he knew, at least in outline, but what he was not yet ready to know was the reason in full. The time for learning this, however, was nearly upon him. Soon he would become the person that he was born to be.

Much later, years in fact after his life-transforming journey, he began to realise that this profound spiritual experience was in fact a sacred rite of passage, preparing him for what lay ahead. Here I beg to mention, dear reader, that such sacred rites of passage, ancient in origin and once a common feature of life, these now are an aspect of the past that is disappearing from the world, such is the lack of value placed on spirituality by contemporary civilisation, and the arrogance of religions that do not know the true nature of God. Oh dear, I have mentioned the desert figurative once again, and also touched upon a matter most profound that lies at the core of that which ails the world!

Back once more to my tale, and it was because of this journey of the soul, and also because he chose to follow the path less well defined in the pursuit of his dreams, that he was eventually confronted with that which he knew lay waiting for him, this being part of his never-ending journey. As for that which lay waiting for him, what was this? The answer is an occurrence that manifested itself in a most difficult, and at many times confusing, life event, where that invisible hand reached out to him one more time, but for a reason that was in his mind, still unclear, although he knew it was entangled, in ways most mysterious, with another person. Here I make clear that this part of our wounded healer's story was not yet over, and that night would see one more turn of the page of this tale, as you will see later in my story. Here is another way-marker.

How much of the night had passed away before he heard the approaching footsteps does not, in my tale, matter. Here in the desert, counting moments in time was of little consequence, there being plenty of time and no need to keep an account of it. The Fair-haired One did not stir, for he knew who approached; it was Hassan.

Hassan had brought with him his own cushions and blankets, announcing to the Fair-haired One, that he, Hassan, intended to stay, to help the Fair-haired One keep vigil that night. No objection was raised by the Fair-haired One, for our stranger, visitor to the desert lands, knew there would be other moments for solitude and silence.

"Comfortable?" Hassan asked, as he began to make to his own liking his chosen resting place for the night, which lay close by the Fair-haired One.

"Very," came the brief reply.

"And what do you make of that new star in the east? A sign perhaps?" Hassan asked.

"Without doubt it is a sign of some significant event, but exactly what? This we shall never know."

"True, but there are stories that foretell the coming of a great healer who will heal the world. Perhaps this star announces the arrival of this person."

"Perhaps, but perhaps not. You speculate. As I said, we will never know."

"Sometimes it is good to speculate, my friend. It helps to bring some understanding to our world."

"Fulfils a human need, you mean?"

"Yes. But it is also the beginning of knowledge, which grows with time as others add to it and reassess that which is known. This is part of the process of life."

Then followed moments of silence as the two of them looked out from their place of rest, eyes wandering, taking in the scene; each with their own thoughts, each also knowing that there was no need to hurry, for the desert night is long and they were not the slaves of time.

The night moved on, and both were silent for the time being, but then Hassan, quite unexpectedly, began to speak of matters most different.

"My friend, you have been with us a few years now."

"Close to two," responded the Fair-haired One.

"I remember well your arrival here," Hassan recalled. "One day you walked out of the desert; an enigmatic stranger from some distant and very different place. I have heard people speak of your lands, far across the sea to the north, where people with fair skins dwell. Then, suddenly, there you were, one of those fair-skinned people, seeking our help. And this we gave you, for we are people of the desert, and we know to be kind to those who choose, for whatever reason, to make the desert their travelling companion. Thus, no hesitation had we in inviting you into our community, of offering you our hospitality, for we know all too well that the desert can easily turn from friend to foe.

"So it was that you sat among us, shared our food, and you in return did that which you could to earn this. People respected you for that, even though they were uncertain about you, and a little suspicious, for these things are quite natural, of course. But they wondered why you, from colder lands, chose to travel the desert at all. And we could not ask you, nor could you tell us, for we did not know at that time how to speak your language, nor you ours. As for myself, I could sense about you a hurting that I have never before seen in a man."

The Fair-haired One was quiet, not wanting here to respond, for he knew his dear friend Hassan very well; knew that Hassan was leading to something important. So he waited, letting Hassan speak his way gently towards the point of the conversation.

"Each day you watched, as we argued among ourselves, about that which must have seemed incomprehensible to you. But, somehow, you knew that which perplexed us. You understood that it was the path up to the higher pastures that was the source of our dissatisfaction, and how we ached because of our impotence to do anything about it.

"Long ago," Hassan continued, "far beyond living memory, when our ancestors first came to this place, they built a path to the greener pastures that lie further up from here. On this higher ground, once the rains have been, there is fine grazing for our sheep. Yet the path that our forefathers made is a very poor one. For certain, it starts well, which may have been why it was built where it is, but it soon becomes difficult and dangerous to traverse, and over countless years we have lost many sheep; those that have lost their footing and fallen to their deaths. Our people too have been hurt at times.

"On numerous occasions we had tried to improve the path, but to no avail, for the problem was far too fundamental for incremental remedies. And every time we made some adaptation, some improvement, we just seemed to make matters worse elsewhere. Thus it was that most had come to realise that we needed a new path, but everywhere we looked, all we could see were places where starting a new trail would be difficult, and no one could see a route for such a path. And most people also did not want to take the risk and start work on constructing something new, even though they knew it was the right course of action, and we ended up once again thinking about how we might improve that which we had, as this seemed easier than starting afresh. We did this in spite of the fact that all knew that a new route to the higher pastures was the right way forward."

Here Hassan paused for a moment, as if mentally preparing himself for that which he wanted to say next, and indeed this is what he was doing. The Fair-haired One knew this and was happy to let the momentary silence be, for silence is good for the soul. Then Hassan began to speak once more.

"In some unfathomable way, you understood all this. At first I did not know how or why, but now I do; you were sent here to show us the way. And this you did, but not in a style that most men would have adopted.

"I know very well the ways of men," Hassan remarked. "Many like to think of themselves as leaders, and this they believe means telling other people what to do, pretending that they know that which is best, and that we should follow them. Yet it is rarely the case that such people do know that which is best. Most often, that which such people seek is their own glorification and the pampering of their egos; they want to feel important. But not you! You acted out of love, for that is all I can see as the reason for what you did, although at first that was not my reaction."

Hassan then began to recall the events that had taken place early one morning close to two years past.

"One morning I rose early, somewhat curious to know what was happening outside for I could hear a noise that sounded like someone at work! I emerged from my tent, and what did I see? The answer, my friend, was you, working on your own, starting to build a new path, in a place that none of us would have even considered as a suitable starting point.

"I must tell you that I was a little angry. 'Why is this stranger building a new path?' I asked myself. 'What business is it of his?' So I was going to stop you, but then something mysterious happened. I paused and listened to that voice inside my head; that quiet voice that speaks to us all the time, but which we often ignore. It was my soul telling me to think again. So I did, and in an instant I had a different perspective: 'If a stranger cares that much about our difficulties that he is willing on his own to start building a new path, then perhaps I should help him.' This is what I thought, and so this is what I did."

"I remember that moment very well," responded the Fair-haired One. "No words passed between us, but we understood each other."

Hassan smiled as he too recalled that instant and warm memories came to mind. The Fair-haired One also smiled, and for a moment the bond existing between these two men would have been obvious to anyone watching them.

"What happened next," Hassan continued, "was even more mysterious. A neighbour came out to see what was happening. He watched for a while, then he asked me, 'Hassan what are you doing?' Thus I told him that if a stranger cared enough to start building a new path, I thought that I should help.

"For a moment there was no response to my reply, then he, too, this neighbour of mine, decided the same, that if you, a stranger, cared enough about our problems to want to try to solve them, then the right course of action was to help.

"So it went on. One by one, people came out from their tents to discover the reason for all the noise, and each joined

in. No more questions were asked; they just followed your example. Soon, all who were able were working to build the new path. Everyone was smiling at you and the suspicion that once my people had for you disappeared. People came to you and patted you on the back or they hugged you. No one spoke, for they knew words were useless. Their actions, though, spoke louder than any words could ever have done. It was as though you had healed our community."

Hassan had now almost finished recounting these events. His final words on this matter related to the outcome of this community endeavour.

"Thus it was that the new path was built. Of course there were moments when we were unsure which direction to take, and a few efforts that led us the wrong way. But together we worked out where the pathway should go. Now, no one can understand why we did not build this new trail long ago, for not only is it far better, but it also leads up past pastures that we would never have been able to use if we had not built this new path, and, as a result, our flocks of sheep are better fed, and everyone is happy with this."

Hassan stopped speaking and waited again; more moments of silence in a world where such silence was the norm, where there was no need to fill every waking second of the day with mindless chatter and activities. Sorry, that other desert, figurative, is once more appearing in my tale, and I did make a promise, did I not?

"It is as you say," the Fair-haired One responded, while also not at all wanting to take credit for this, for he knew that it was important not to; this, you must understand, is the way of a wounded healer. "But all I did was to make a start, to give you the confidence that finding a new path was possible. After that, what you did, you did yourselves. This is the *power of one*; it can change anything! Plant the seed of a tree today, and next year there is a young sapling, but in a hundred years, though, there may be a small wood, and in a thousand years, a forest. This is how we can transform and heal the world. No one needs to be hurt and no one has to die to create a better place for all. Someone just needs to say, 'that which is now will be no more', and to peacefully start making this so. The climate of thought will eventually begin to change and others will start to see the value and join in. Whatever you call the better world that you seek, your paradise, you cannot build a kingdom of heaven on ground that is soaked in the blood of people who do not agree with you. There can be no compulsion. In the end it is love that will overpower and change those that are doubtful, those that resist, those who wish to maintain the world as it is. Love will render the powerful powerless, and turn the table, so that it is no longer those who seek to change the world who will have to justify themselves, but those who would hold on to orthodoxy."

Here I intervene once more, dear reader, to tell you that not only is this a way-marker, but the foundation upon which you should base your life and build the future; become a wounded healer, for all are wounded and all have the choice to transform their pain into that which will make the world a better place.

"This is what I like about you, my dear friend –" responded Hassan – "always modest about that which you have done, what you have achieved, and very spiritual as well. You have wisdom. These are good traits. Very endearing! Keep them. They will serve you and the world well. But, if you will forgive me to ask, why did you come here?"

"You have answered that question yourself, Hassan. I was sent here."

"Ah, yes. But that is not the meaning of my question, and well you know it. Never have you spoken about your reasons for travelling across the desert, and even now, when we can communicate with one another, no one asks out for respect for you and that which you did for us."

The Fair-haired One remained silent, unsure of what to say, for he did not want to speak of this matter, but neither did he wish to cause offence by avoiding answering Hassan's question.

Hassan could see that his friend was hesitating and uncertain how to respond, so he said that which he felt sure was the reason. "Was it because of a woman? Is this the cause of your hurt?"

This seemed to hit the target well, for it was indeed because of a woman that the Fair-haired One sat where he now did. "Yes," came the reply. "This is why I came here, but she is not the cause of that which you call my hurt. I would not call it such, for it is a wounding, inflicted for a purpose, but of this I do not wish to speak at the moment, other than to say that this belongs to an aspect of being that is deep and profound, yet, in an enigmatic way, the wounding and the fair lady are bound together, for they are part of the same."

Then more silence as the Fair-haired One thought and wondered what to impart to Hassan by way of additional information. And Hassan waited patiently.

"It is very complicated," continued the Fair-haired One.

"Matters concerning relationships between men and women often are complicated," interjected Hassan. "She is married? Yes? And very beautiful? And you mention something that I do not understand, and you will not speak of it. This is very mysterious."

"Yes, Hassan, she is married and beautiful, but that is not what I meant when I said it was complicated. As for the other matter, please do not ask, for now is not the moment to share this with you. One day, perhaps I will explain, if, that is, it is your destiny to know about this."

"Very well then, I will not push you on this matter. But, that which is even more complicated than she being a beautiful married woman! This you must try to explain, for I am intrigued. I cannot imagine anything more complex than that which I have already mentioned."

"Well, my friend, the strangeness of my life is beyond comprehension. Believe me, that which I experienced lies outside the realm of this mortal world, being also full of meaning and purpose, and, as I said, is connected with a special event in my life of a spiritual nature."

"So I am beginning to perceive that what you are experiencing is not of earthly origins. It is not affairs of the heart which drove you away from this fair woman, but of the soul. Yes, that makes sense to me, given the way you helped us. Matters here, I think, of unfathomable complexity at work."

"My friend, unfathomable complexity is a good phrase to describe that which has happened, for it is, beyond all doubt, unfathomable. This is why I came to the desert, to seek solitude and silence so that I might better understand my experiences and their meaning. But when I say that I came to the desert, it was not I think by choice, as it seems to me that I was led here, almost as if to ensure that I would not be near to this fair and angelic woman."

"Then fate has brought you to the right place, for here in the desert we are attuned to matters unfathomably complex. As for solitude and silence, this too is the place, as I note you have taken good advantage of. So tell me, what exactly did you encounter to make you turn from, or which led you from, your own lands, to seek comfort and shelter so far way from home?"

"I said she is beautiful. Indeed she is, but there is an aspect to her beauty that does not refer to her appearance, for she has what I would call a beautiful soul. Then that invisible and familiar hand reached out to me, and, speaking in silence, told me to take note of this, as if to say, 'Look who is standing next to you.' So I looked. And if it had not been for this, I would have walked away, and kept on walking. But I could not. From that moment on it was as though our souls had become as one."

Here, dear reader, I will interject one more time, for which I beg your forgiveness, but here is one of those way-markers. Note it well for it has a bearing on this story, its meaning and its outcome. Now let me continue with my tale.

"A beautiful soul! An unusual turn of phrase for something that is, indeed, a very precious and special gift, but do go on. I can see why you refer to her as angelic. Tell me more."

"There is but one word that describes this, and that is love; not though love of the type that we as people are used to experiencing. No, this love was pure and beyond this world, and at times it overwhelms me, in a way that romantic love never did, nor, I think, ever could. For you see, even though I am far away, and this special person has been out of sight for well on two years now, I feel this love everywhere I go, and every day. It will not leave me alone, and it is as though it is calling to me, yet I know not what to do, for it comes with nothing that makes sense to me, yet, as I have hinted, seems part of me and related to that which lies in my past."

A tear at this point found its way from the Fair-haired One's right eye, and slowly, and quite on its own, meandered its way down his cheek, eventually falling from his face to become lost in the world. Hassan, watching, smiled.

"My friend! My dear friend, you are most blessed, but I dare say that you think not."

"Blessed is not a word that I would use. Cursed perhaps, but not blessed."

"Yes, I can see why you might think that but, let me tell you, what you have just said also speaks to me of a different kind of love to that which normally exists between man and woman. About this I think you are right. This is not romantic love. I will try to explain."

The Fair-haired One said nothing by way of response, but just glanced towards Hassan, slightly nodding to communicate that he was listening, and curious to know more.

"I am a desert shepherd," Hassan continued. "I spend many nights alone with my sheep. This has given me much time to think, to reflect, to come to know my inner self.

And of course, while I stay out with my sheep, the love of my life, she stays at home looking after our children. At night I often think about them, and also about the nature of love that enables me to do that which I do, for without our sheep we would have no means of living, but this love, at the same time, binds us together, keeps us as one, keeps her always in my mind.

"Thinking about such matters over many long years, I have come to the conclusion that there are indeed many types of love. There is that which exists between man and woman, that which finds expression in physical intimacy, but there is another kind of love that we have for one another, that has nothing to do with the physical. It is expressed each day in the care we demonstrate for one another, in all those helping acts we do, because we know that we need one another, and life for us all is better when our actions are guided by this."

The Fair-haired One listened intently as Hassan spoke these words of wisdom about the nature of love, but as yet he had heard nothing that he had not already realised himself from his own experiences. What Hassan said next, however, was a revelation.

"My friend, I believe also that there is another type of love, much rarer and far more precious than any love that normally exists between two people. It is a love that most have forgotten, and which few are now able to sense and respond to. It is extraordinarily potent, to a degree beyond comprehension, bringing with it the power to transform the world. This love of which I speak is divine love, whose source lies beyond the universe, and you my friend may have encountered this! So I say again, you are indeed blessed."

"When you say beyond the universe, you mean …"

"Unfathomable complexity. Yes, my friend, I do."

"But why is this divine love linked to such a fair and beautiful woman, and a married one at that? This is what perplexes me."

"That, my friend, is the nature of unfathomable complexity, and you must seek to understand why, for it will not be told to you in the form of a simple answer. This, one might say, is a tale as old as time in more ways than one, being bound up in love that transcends the mortal, this divine love, while also at the same time being grounded in that which seems to be just one more tale of hearts' desires. Yet the former, this divine love, may need the other, the romantic love, for the latter is more simple to understand, and becomes the stepping stone that leads one to the door of that love which is beyond the realms of humankind. Yet to understand this means putting aside that which is born of reason, that which comes from the logic of the mind, and learning to listen to the voice of one's soul. The trail that leads to this understanding is there for you both to follow; the choice for each of you is not whether to undertake this quest, but when. This experience, this encounter, is a way-marker, left for you both to find, so that together you will be able to follow this path."

"This is what I meant when I said matters are complex," responded the Fair-haired One. "This is not at all easy. How can one be sure of this?"

"You cannot," Hassan said in response. "All you can do is to trust in your intuition. This is the way that is difficult to walk, where the road to follow is less clear, which will lead you to a beautiful place. You must listen to the voice of your soul, not of your mind, for that is too rational and logical to understand any of this. Please also take note that in matters such as this, being wrong is not the issue, for the mind will always tell you that you are mistaken. Your soul knows better and also understands the price of not following the path, and will therefore not give up until you take note of that which it is telling you. Let me also say that this love has already changed the world, for it has brought you to us, and … well, we have already mentioned here tonight the result of this."

Hassan fell silent, giving time for the Fair-haired One to reflect, not wanting to push him further if he was not ready to hear that which Hassan wanted to say next, for he was hoping that he would not need to say it, and that the Fair-haired One would come to the conclusion himself.

They sat in silence, but for how long is of no concern, for, as I have already told you, here in the desert, time did not matter. When the Fair-haired One was ready, there would be a response to Hassan. So time passed by, yet the night still had many long hours left in it.

"I think you are telling me that it is time to leave, and to return to where she dwells," the Fair-haired One eventually said.

Hassan nodded his agreement.

"But surely people would misunderstand."

"Yes, there will be those who will misunderstand, and even condemn; people who live their lives by rules, who only talk in terms of that which thou shalt not do, without even trying to understand why, or to ask if that which seems black and white might just be grey, or is done for love, without thought of gain, pleasure or some darker objective. Such people, such believers, are always a problem. These individuals are very dangerous, both to themselves and to others. They are the ones who seek only a destination, and miss the point that it is the journey that matters, and that there are as many journeys as there are people. They will not look to see that which appears before them, but will make judgement based on ignorance and call upon higher authority in the process to justify themselves. They, above all others, do not seek an understanding of the nature of unfathomable complexity, nor do they realise that in the end there can be no destination, for journeys towards infinity never end. My friend, do not let these people hold you back. It may be the least of your worries. The fair woman herself may be the biggest challenge!"

"What do you mean?" the Fair-haired One asked.

"Do you think that you are alone in experiencing these feelings? That cannot be. She too must have encountered this divine love, and perhaps, also like you, is confused and wondering what she should do. She may be torn; pulled one way towards he whom she loves, and also towards you, but for reasons she does not know, or which she assumes are to do with her heart. She may even be a little fearful, despite there being nothing to fear. Perhaps her instinct is to turn away from you, to banish you from her life, thinking that time will heal that which she thinks is a rupture to her heart. And indeed it would, if it was in fact romantic love, for time is a great healer. But the truth is that no amount of time will heal that which you have both encountered, as I think you have already come to realise. I believe, from that which you have said, that your life, and that of this fair woman, are not intended to be united in the sense of two lives lived as one. You will discover, I think, that there are aspects of your destinies that are shared in common, entangled, maybe not now, but perhaps at some future point in your lives, possibly even after you, my friend, have left this world. No one can know, but this is what you need to explore, and together, to find that common destiny. But I will tell you that it must be something very important, and knowing you as I do – you the pathfinder, you the pathmaker – this I think may be a clue. So now we are back where we started; with that star burning bright in the east."

This final statement came as a surprise to the Fair-haired One, who did not see the connection. "With the star, what do you mean?" the Fair-haired One asked.

"Yes, my friend. Well may it be that this star is a sign of the coming of a very special person, who will begin to heal the world. But to do that means that we all have to change, to work on such a task, and to become healers ourselves. And who more fitting than you, a person with a wounded soul – a pathfinder, a pathmaker, a wounded healer – to be the one who shows the way?"

"I can do no more here; I must leave. This is the end. This is farewell. This is the beginning. This is the journey that has no end. Somehow I must find a way of gently sharing with this beautiful person, all that you have said, so that she can begin to understand," responded the Fair-haired One.

"Yes, most definitely."

"And if she rejects this, what do I do?"

"You must be patient and wait," Hassan began to explain. "If necessary you must wait for years, for battles between the soul and the mind can go on for a long time. She, in the end, must be the one to decide, and in her own time. Know this, however: her soul will not give up, will not let her forget you, and will keep you in her mind, constantly reminding her that she has an appointment with her destiny. And you must always be there for her, so that in the end, when she does decide, she will be able to speak to you."

"This I will do. I will always be there for her, always ready to speak with her. But when she begins to understand, and starts to accept, and then asks me for what purpose. What do I say?"

"You tell her about the desert. You tell that here, here in this world, among all this aridness, there are places called oases, where there is water and lush vegetation, and great beauty. Yet words can never truly communicate what such places are like. Only by visiting an oasis can one really understand it and that which it represents in the desert. Yet to reach such an understanding one has to make the journey, which often involves many hardships, and it is by making such a journey that one gains insights concerning the beauty of the destination, which is not a point of termination, but just one more staging post on the journey."

"The path will be hard! The way unclear!" the Fair-haired One said.

"Yes, for certain. That is why you should both walk it. You are engaged in a divine dance of love, and therefore you will find the way, for it is part of your destinies to do so, and in doing this you will become that which you truly are, what you were born to be. And so will she!"

~

Thus it was that the Fair-haired One came to realise that his time in the desert was drawing to a close. The waiting was over. Now coming was a challenging journey, and once more it would be along the way that is most difficult to walk, where the road to follow is less clear. This is the journey that has no end, that has no final destination, but which will lead one to beautiful places.

That night he also came to understand a little bit more about himself, for if indeed Hassan was correct, that he had encountered love divine, then there must be a profoundly important reason for this, which lay within both him and this person with the beautiful soul, and be connected to that which each had already experienced. They needed not only to find the path, but also to discover why they had had such an encounter in the first place, and how this was linked to their pasts.

Concerning this profoundly important reason just referred to, somehow, and in some unfathomable way, he knew this lay in a distant future, in a place that had, in a figurative sense, become a desert, where the world of unfathomable complexity wrought by the hand of unfathomable complexity would be no more, at least in the minds of many men! This of course did not mean that it was no more, just that men, in their delusions, both individual and collective, denied such matters. Yet the hand is indeed unfathomable because the delusions may in the end be but part of the unfathomable complexity; humankind's own collective journey towards its destiny.

The End

Another Desert

There is more here than just words, and more to the words than just mere words; and of deserts, what can be said? Here now find, in words spoken in silence, learning, understanding, and wisdom, for deserts are places where life prospers, even though at times it can seem to some, those perhaps who judge too much based on appearances, that there is no life. Yet there are deserts, not of natural origin you must understand, where life most definitely does not flourish. Yet even in such places, there is still hope for life.

To this matter I turn, to deserts figurative, where unfolds this rather strange tale in a world that is no more enigmatic, for not here will you find talk of unfathomable complexity, as in this place all can be known; it is just a matter of time.

Here there is no room for the spiritual, and nothing here is sacred. This is a world which offers a cold and pointless vision of the universe, where purpose is not needed, and people are just machines who in the end will also not be needed. This is a world of final destinations without journeys, where minds have closed in on fixed opinions, and where there is also much need for healing, such is the lunacy that can be found everywhere; in science, technology, engineering, religion, and business.

This is the hell to which man in his folly condemns himself, and all in the name of science and the pursuit of matters economic and material. And what more materialistic a time of year is there than Christmas? This, you see, is the importance of money in the materialistic world, where life is significantly improved at the cost of everything that matters most. Here, nothing is of value unless it has economic value.

But do not worry, for you have your delusions; that place of sanctuary to which you can retreat in the face of unpalatable truths. Yet, even here, reality has a nasty habit of finding its way into your mind, as you will see as my tale unfolds. So perhaps there is still hope. Now, as you with little time would expect, the scene is briefly set for that which follows.

~

'Tis Christmas Eve once more! And being that wintry time of year, snow, freshly fallen from the heavens, covers the streets, the gardens, the rooftops and the fields. It looks as though some mysterious hand has painted the landscape white, but there is no such hand; it is just nature at work, doing that which can be predicted.

This white blanket transforms the otherwise bleak and drab-brown winter landscape, which, as we know, is largely devoid of the brilliant colours that other seasons bring. This is just a fact of nature, and there is no need to make anything of it; just facts, that is all. I am sure you understand and approve!

Cold are the long nights, as are the short days. The moon, earth's cosmic partner, waxing towards fullness, on the brink of a full revelation, shines intensely in the otherwise ink-black night sky. Stars that normally twinkle bright cannot compete with the moonshine, and thus remain hidden from earthly view, but nevertheless they still sparkle, even though unseen. And the snow, reflecting this silver moonlight, creates a ghostly white scene out of which those still inclined to engage in that which some would call mystical nonsense might easily imagine a Christmas spectre to suddenly appear. Thankfully, or perhaps not, we now live in an age where facts and not imagination prevails! Time moved on. Progress, as they say, was made. The world, the solar system, the universe – these became defined only by knowledge that can be proven by experiment. There is no alternative, or so it is believed. Such are the values that underlie beliefs – something else that lies unseen! Every era has its myths! You think that this does not apply to your own time, this age of science and technology? You do indeed deceive yourself!

I imagined a dream and I dreamed of worlds that are, and also of worlds that could be. And I dreamed that a bird, a creature of the natural world, found its way into a place of man's making, and, not wanting to be there, desired to leave, but was unable to do so, even though the way out was clear. For some reason it was frightened to return, but was also fearful to stay, and thus it became paralysed, caught between two worlds. And I dreamed that I set free this bird, not by capturing it and taking it to the place where it belonged, but by showing it that there was nothing to fear, for the way back was clear and free of all dangers.

This is the power of dreams; sacred places where the spiritual can still enter our minds, gently or not so gently, depending on the need, trying to teach us that which many no longer have an inclination to learn. Thus it is that knowledge has become impoverished, and man, boldly striding forward in the delusion that his knowledge and understanding grows, in fact retreats towards greater ignorance. Yet dreams, they still speak to us; we should listen! So sleep now and dream.

Thus it was that time moved on for all souls. The world turned, another year passed, and one cold December became yet another one and, as always, watched were all and all were watched. For standing there in the darkness, at the edge of vision, where few care to look, was a watcher whom you and everyone else would do well to fear and keep out of your life, and yet also, there, fully in the light, was another observer, who no deception uses.

Who are these beings of whom I speak?

Across all the ages of man, people have given these creatures names, yet most of these are lost to memory, such are the ancient origins of these entities. In the medieval mind they were demons and angels. One, the first that is, a demon who is in essence a fallen angel, a dark angel, full of malevolence, and the other, being the second of course, a true angel, part of the light. And in modern times, what now does humankind call these immortal life forms? Why nothing, for no names are needed, because they are, it is confidently proclaimed, nothing but a superstition, an invention of minds that did not know the truth. Yet still they watch!

Evil works in many ways; it does not need to pour forth from the twisted mind, delivering hatred, greed, death, and destruction to a world already drowning in these terrible things. Other ways, more subtle and more insidious, have been found to add to humanity's woes, and perhaps none more so than that which can be found in he who knows the truth, but in reality knows only a deception, but being deceived, believes he knows the truth. Delusions you must understand, both individual and collective, are mankind's great weakness; his flaw and the key to his downfall. Blindness to this is everywhere, for those who are blind to this truth, being blind, cannot see they are blind.

'Tis Christmas Eve once more! I know I repeat myself, but this is an important detail, so note it well, for its bearing on that which follows makes of my story, towards its end, full sense. Now of course you wonder at my meaning, but hold steady, do not become too curious, be patient, and, in due course, all will be revealed. Thus repeating myself further, one more time I beg your tolerance, when I say that one cold December has become yet another one. The days of the year passed by, one by one. Our small world, this sacred place we call home, this majestic planet on which we live, has orbited the bright burning sun, coming back to just about the same place it was one year previously. Not exactly the same, you will note, for nothing can be entirely as it was, if only in some minuscule way, by virtue of some slight variation, which can make all the difference.

In an eternal, repeating story, the dark days of December change to the dark days of January, both being months full of gloom. But slight changes are afoot as, imperceptibly at first, the darkness starts to give way to the light. Thus it is that as the days lengthen, the night begins its retreat, and soon spring is upon us, bringing new life among the bright green colours of the season. Then warmth gradually and stealthily tiptoes its way in, driving away those harsh memories of cold and dull winter days, until at last they are well forgotten and we all bask in the full glory of summer. Yet time, being relentless, never stops, and so the days begin once more to grow short, and the brightness of the mid-year time gives way to autumn's golden splendour, occasionally choosing to remind us of the glorious season just past, by offering, here and there, balmy fall days when the sun, no longer at its zenith, does its best to fulfil its purpose, to provide those that dwell on planet earth with the warmth and light that makes life possible. And see, that was not too hard – to think, that is, in terms of purpose, rather than just solely in terms of cause and effect, that soulless and barren concept that has done so much damage to man's perceptions of himself, nature and the universe.

But do not be fooled by warm autumn days and the golden light that they bring. They may seem to be reassuring, a comfort to all, but as sure as the sun will rise and set, so it is with the coming of winter, for arrive it must and with it goes the delusion that may have taken root in the minds of men, that this will not be so. Winter will come, and show them all that this is reality, and no amount of dressing up with fine words can change this fact. Yet it is a pity that this is not so with other delusions that have taken hold of the minds of men, especially those people who are products of the modern era, who see no need for that which comes from times that they mistakenly see as being more primitive and less sophisticated!

Thus the planets proceed along their orbits, but no longer is this the harmony of the spheres, but just an effect, resulting from some cause, obeying well-defined laws; just beautiful equations devoid of purpose, for there is no longer room for this. Not here will you find an unfathomable complexity shaped by the hand of unfathomable complexity. In the end, the universe is what it is and has no reason to be, and there being no cause for its existence, all one can say is that it just happened, for the trail of causes in the end dries up. It is not necessary to explain. Of course, this line of argument would not be accepted for any other aspect of scientific study – everything has a cause until, that is, the power of science is shown, in the limit, to have limits. Then one resorts to that which for every other matter in science would not be accepted; it is not necessary to explain why the universe exists – it just does. Problem resolved? More like problem denied! And still they watch!

On this bright Christmas Eve night, the moon, also an orbiting celestial body, is moving, imperceptibility of course on the timescale of one night, yet it moves! But its motion is unlike that of the planets, big and small, since for the moon, our moon, the earth is indeed its centre; the hub of its perpetual dance with its partner earth! Perhaps, therefore – I beg you, dear reader, to reflect upon this – it is not difficult to imagine, given this simple observation, how man in times past might have come to the conclusion that the earth did not move, and that all heavenly bodies around the earth did proceed, and that all in fact was quite small, reassuringly so, with a clear boundary where that which is the universe came to an end.

Yet it moves! is what Galileo supposedly said – I did say that all ages have their myths, did I not? Yet still they watch!

And of these myths, what more can be said? What final words before proceeding with my tale? Only one, I beg your patience, and it is this – that man discovered the truth and gave birth to the modern era – the age of science, the dominion of facts, evidence, and reason; but other truths became forgotten because men's minds lost the ability to comprehend them. As I said, man's intellect recedes. And yet still they watch!

Which truths? you ask. You are of course, dear reader, most likely a person conditioned by the culture of modernity; a child of Newton and his clockwork universe, no longer able to fully perceive, such is the result of the intellectual conditioning that passes for education and personal development in this lunatic asylum called the modern age. Here then, briefly, is your answer: the truth is that we, the world, and the universe, are more than just physical matter and there are many ways, equally valid, of understanding these things, and each of these ways is complementary and not competing. Each can reinforce the other, and lead to a world that is not a lunatic asylum, if we have but the wisdom to see this. Wisdom, however, is a human trait that is increasingly absent from the contemporary world.

Long ago, you may be surprised to learn, the Ancient Greeks reached an understanding that the universe (or, more accurately, the solar system) is heliocentric but they subsequently, as their civilisation began to collapse, retreated back to more familiar, more reassuring thoughts of a geocentric universe, finite and walled-in. So, I ask, where will your mind retreat to when your own civilisation collapses, as inevitably it will? Perhaps you do not need to retreat for you have already done so, swapping a walled-in universe for a walled-in mind, where all is reassuringly familiar and ultimately knowable, where there is no need for God, for soul, for imagination, for ... And so, in their mental, self-constructed prison, the scientists, the technologists, the engineers, they dream no more, for they have created a universe where such human ways of engaging with the world are not required, and that which cannot be explained is of no importance, for such does not exist. Yet it does exist. Yet they watch! But I digress. Did I not tell you 'tis Christmas Eve, and to note this well?

On this snowy Christmas Eve to which I have drawn your attention, trudging through the snow comes Richard; one of scientific inclination, an icon of contemporary civilisation.

For one so young, being that is a man in his late twenties, the snow and ice pose no problems for Richard. He is not at all impeded and he boldly pushes forward as though exploring a new frontier, no longer concerned about the need for caution. And if he were to slip, to fall, it would only be as an afterthought, might he be so lucky, that he would suggest proceeding with more caution. Yet we all know that this would not last, for man it seems no more understands this notion, and will do that which science demands. Oh Epimetheus! It does not matter that you choose to call yourself Richard or a thousand other names in all the languages of the world; whatever you may choose as a name for yourself is irrelevant, for you are Epimetheus and are indeed well named.

Richard makes his way along the snow-covered pavements. And being a moonlit night, with the world around blanketed in pure white snow, the lack of street lighting in the small village where he dwells causes no difficulties and he can see, very clearly, the path he must follow towards his destination, about which I will have more to say shortly. And, as I said, for Richard it is an effortless trail to follow, so no thoughts enter his mind concerning alternative paths; there is only the one best way and to this we are committed. There is no alternative.

Being also Christmas, the yuletide season, that time of year when being jolly is the main preoccupation, the small shops that line the road in the centre of the village, being as they are engines of economic activity, are decorated in the seasonal style, offering widow displays designed to entice, helping to generate, for many, that festive atmosphere, creating at an otherwise drab and dismal time of year a colourfulness that nature is not able to provide. And there in these windows are the familiar symbols of Christmas time: the green garlands, the sprigs of holly, the multi-coloured festive lights, pretty tinsel, baubles both decorated and plain, miniature Christmas trees adorned with many decorative items, cute little animals bearing Christmas hats and scarves, Santas and reindeer, and, of course, nativity scenes. This latter element is what Christmas is all about, although for many this is no longer so, for that which happened two thousand years past is not anymore of much interest. Spirituality, you must understand, increasingly has no place in the modern world, and few are able to see how this impoverishes us all and the activities in which we engage. You will note, dear reader, that I did refer to spirituality and not to religion! There is a big difference, as we all can see, when those of religious inclination demonstrate their ignorance of the true nature of God by killing, or hurting, or persecuting those they do not like or agree with. God, it seems, is easily offended, or is it the religious man in his delusions that is insulted, while God, being God, takes no offence at all?

Richard continues on his way, moving past the traditional images of Christmas, not taking much notice of them. Then suddenly there are no window displays, just a wide gap, a place where buildings of commerce do not exist, before once more starts another row of shops. And in this gap, this place undisturbed by the making of money, set well back from the road, stands the village church, which is alive with activity.

Being Christmas Eve (remember I told you to note this well), the sights and sounds of Christmas are all about this religious building, this setting for worship of a God not now often discussed in the mainstream of life. This is the nature of deserts manmade.

Drifting through the open door comes the sound of a choir singing, with one accord, Christmas carols, "Oh little town of Bethlehem, How still we see they lie ..." and then, a few minutes later, "Hark the herald angels sing, Glory to the new born King ..." and so on, time slipping by for those willing to pause their journey and take in this Christmas choral harmony. Through this open door also spills out light from within, and stood close by the entrance is a large Christmas tree, decorated as tradition demands, with lights, baubles and tinsel, as one often sees in such public spaces. Light, as well, streams from the stained-glass windows, projecting coloured patterns on to the whiteness of the snow-covered ground; yet more of those red and green colours that are the trademark of the season. And finally, in the graveyard – the place that many now think of as final journey's end, with no thought at all that life's journeys never end – close by the path, completing this perfect picture of Christmas, also stands a nativity scene.

Richard had paused for a moment to survey all this, slightly turning his head towards the church, but only for a moment, for quickly he turned away again, as these aspects of Christmas were of no interest to him, and he fixed his gaze once more to the fore, ready to continue on his way. And ahead of him, a man, who had not been there before! Recall it is Christmas Eve!

Richard, now motionless, spoke quietly to himself. "Where did you come from?" he enquired of himself, for the sudden appearance of this stranger did not fit with that which had been before his eyes a second or two previously.

Richard's logical mind, dominated as it was by cause and effect, was alert to such matters, being also a mind accustomed to observation, yet not seeing.

The effect was clear enough to Richard – a man on the pavement ahead of him, walking away from the spot where Richard stood close by the church. The stranger was evidently old, for he seemed quite small, and walked with a shuffle while bent forward, and in his right hand a walking cane to steady his balance. Yes, clearly an old man.

But what of the cause? Where had this fellow appeared from? Perhaps he had been standing in a recessed doorway admiring a window display, or maybe he had emerged from one of the shops. Yes, surely one of these was the explanation, the cause. So the slight bemusement that had momentarily afflicted Richard's brain was gone, and he resumed walking, moving forwards, continuing with his journey.

He reached the place where the old man had been when he, Richard that is, had first noticed him, the old man, for that the man was old was now, to Richard, a clear and proven conclusion. That which would come next, inspection at close quarters, so to speak, would only prove this by way of additional observational evidence.

Curiously though, there were no recessed doorways where someone could stand and lurk unseen by a person further along the street, and all the shops were closed, locked, and empty, for the selling of Christmas goods was over; all the food, gifts, decorations, cards, and many other items, all products of the consumer age, being those which, at Christmas time, shopkeepers want to sell, and people want to buy. Christmas items that, it can be observed, often are not needed, being as they are part of that process of diffusion of comfort and prosperity that comes from the stimulation of demand and growth, yet which no one dares ask if such can be continued in this traditional form, given the self-evident damage that this is causing to the natural world.

It did not take long for Richard to notice, also, that the trail of footsteps which the elderly gentleman had left in the freshly fallen covering of snow – the virgin layer, lying upon that which had arrived earlier that day – that these marks left by each slow step, well they just started in the middle of the pavement. No links to a doorway could be seen, and that, Richard acknowledged to himself, was just plain odd. But fortunately, Richard, being of a scientific orientation, was not one to engage in mystical or superstitious explanations. There was a logical, physical and rational explanation for this, as for everything, and the matter was of no importance, so he gave it no further thought, continuing on his way as though nothing had happened. Oh to be so sophisticated as to be able to dismiss that which does not have a place in that which masquerades as rational thought!

Now time, especially for a young and fit person, does not much pass by when moving between one place and another that are not very far apart. So it was only a few brief moments before Richard caught up with what, to Richard, seemed to be a very decrepit man. Richard passed him in an instant, and would have left this stranger far behind very rapidly, had not that which I will now recount to you taken place.

"A fine Christmas Eve to be out and about young man," the stranger said in a clear and loud voice. "Would you be so kind as to help an ageing fellow human?" he enquired, continuing with this rather sudden, unexpected, and from Richard's perspective, unwanted verbal engagement on the part of one stranger towards another. And curious as well, since for a person to refer to himself as a fellow human was, to say the least, an unusual turn of phrase.

This was the beginning of a very bizarre encounter for Richard; one of those potentially life-changing meetings. Only in potential though, for not all are able to reap the full benefits of such latent opportunities – first one has to recognise the potential, which for those who call themselves scientists (as well as those who would be known as engineers or technologists) is more difficult than many appreciate.

Richard, being a very modern man, did not want to stop, or to be drawn into a conversation with a person who, he instantly assumed, was a lonely old man seeking solace through social contact with a passing stranger. But the old fellow had asked for help, so it would have been very impolite in such a small place as this village, where some residue of compassion, neighbourliness, and empathy towards one's fellow humans still remained, to ignore this simple request. Ah, yes, simple requests! How often they are far from simple, at least in terms of consequences. Like a small stone cast into a still pond; how those ripples spread, creating a disturbance where before all was quiet and serene.

But halt Richard did, for some humanity was still to be found here, and he turned around and looked at the stranger, wanting to say no, but unable to do so. This is life! How often we do things by habit, by convention, not thinking for ourselves, preferring familiar patterns and behaviour to that which is truly new and unknown? And quite right, for social conventions are important, but perhaps also sometimes very dangerous, especially when they lead to actions that had better be avoided, or when they close minds to greater truths.

What did our hero of the modern world, our scientist, see before him? It was indeed a picture of a person, almost ancient, or at least it appeared so, yet realism being that which it is, evidently, a fellow whose younger days lay close to 80 years past. This, I must say, was just an assumption on Richard's part, for the stranger could have been far older, perhaps actually ancient in origin, but such a thought would not have occurred to Richard, with his mind being as it was – closed in on fixed opinions.

The person before Richard had not, judging by appearances, aged well at all, for the stranger's face was heavily wrinkled, unusually so. The sight that Richard beheld was that of a wizened man, his skin being like that of a walnut, with wrinkles, creases, and lumps all over his face. As for his hair and beard, these were white as the virgin snow. His eyes were sharp and blue, and these spoke of age, but they also suggested a kindness, for there was warmth about them that alluded to affection and good cheer, and not the hardness and cold cynical bitterness that can sometimes be found among those of advancing years. Being a cold night, there was also some colour about the man's face, for he had rosy red cheeks and a very red nose, where Jack Frost had been busy nipping at the skin, but not yet too much to turn the colour to blue.

"I am a very old man," he continued in a slightly pleading tone. "The snow … it impedes my progress. A helping hand, some support to steady and guide my way, would not be unappreciated, especially from one as strong as you. As you see, I am past my best."

Not waiting for a response, the old man transferred his walking cane from his right hand to his left with a certainty that did not go unnoticed, as if he were very sure of himself and accustomed to such actions. Steadying himself by leaning towards his left side, he then held out his right arm in a manner which did not leave Richard with any choice but to comply. Compliance was here demanded by actions not words, and he fell in line with this, not raising any verbal objections. This also is life, for many comply when they had better speak out and say, 'Oh no, I shall not do that.' Here, however, he was right not to say such words, but that cannot always be said of people such as Richard. Understanding when to say no is something that he and his fellow scientists have yet to learn, and represents a level of sophistication far more important than any theory or experiment.

For one so old, this stranger had a grip that was sure and firm, revealing more strength in this feeble frame than was to be expected from such an elderly gentleman. One of life's many unexpected twists and turns! What would the world be without them? Predictable, boring, known!

Slowly and cautiously, together, and in step, the pair advanced, the pace determined by the older in years, each footstep small in comparison with the bold strides that Richard was used to making. Perhaps one day, Richard too would become accustomed to moving more slowly and cautiously, for all are destined to age, and for some, those who survive to their eighties, their nineties, this is the norm – as is the lack of value that society places on the elderly.

Death will eventually come to all. At some point the Hand of Time will let loose its grip, and all will then be free to fly towards the arms of God. That life will end is inescapable, and we all hope that the coming of this concluding point in our story will be peaceful and serene, like the setting of the sun at the end of a long and balmy summer's day, leaving us with good, warm and pleasant memories of a day well spent and enjoyed. Those of certain religious inclinations hope that they will make their final journey without the devil on their back. These two perspectives may just be different ways of expressing the same thing – die well and at peace with oneself. Yet, less so in these modern times are people aware that such is more likely if the days of one's life are lived in the spirit of love for other living creatures, not just our own kind, but also those other creatures without which human life on earth would not be possible. Love is everything, but its absence from the modern world grows more noticeable as each day passes; yet few speak out about the consequences of this folly. Life it seems is lived increasingly as though it were just a single day, with nothing lying beyond. When the sun sets, it sets. End! Yet, a setting sun is also a shining sun and at the same time also a rising sun; life, the world, the universe are far more complex than they at first appear, being an unfathomable complexity shaped by the hand of unfathomable complexity. To deny this is of no avail, for it still remains an eternal truth.

I am digressing and should therefore now return to my story, which we can resume at a scene where Richard and the elderly stranger have just halted, not because Richard had wanted to, or requested it, but because they had reached a shop window that fascinated the old man. It was obvious why, for it would remind all but the most cold hearted of days long past when the cares of the world were carried by others, and when we were all free to indulge our imagination. I am of course referring here to that wonderful time in our lives we know as childhood. Do you remember those carefree days? Do you recall Christmas time, that best and most delightful period of the year for all children? Christmas and childhood are forever bound together, inseparable memories to which, every Christmas, we all should return. But do we?

"This one's my favourite," he informed Richard, pointing with his cane to the display of toys behind the glass, adding, "it is the shop I look forward most to seeing every Christmas Eve."

"You mean that you do this every Christmas Eve?" Richard asked with a tone of incredulity, and unable now to resist being drawn into a conversation with this eccentric fellow; old, yet in some mysterious way not so old!

"Why yes, of course," came the reply. "For longer than I can remember," he added with a note of delight. "This is what Christmas is about; the giving of gifts. And who are more worthy of gifts than our innocent children? Presents, given in love, in those very precious moments when, with our loved ones gathered about us, we are able to show our love through the sacred act of giving. A very special day my friend, very special indeed! Make the most of such times, young man, for without doubt they will one day come to an end. Then what? What comfort will your science give you at the end of your days, when, like all who have gone before, you face perhaps the most important stage of your journey through life? Man's days are short in this world; make the most of them and hold not to that which limits your experience of the world. Life is a journey, one best made and most fruitful if your eyes are open."

Richard had no time for philosophical reflections, which, one can say, is part of the problem of such people of the modern world. Perhaps if they did have time for philosophy, and art, and literature, and spirituality, they might not be so blind to the damage that they do; they might also be wise, which is something that scientists are, with very few exceptions, most definitely not!

Richard, like many people, thought most seasonal sentiments overly idealistic, and the cynical streak within him, that harsh and unemotional conception of the world in terms of hard facts and the surety that human nature is predominantly exploitative, made him instantly see only the financial gain for those for whom Christmas was a time to make money. But he said nothing of this to the old man, who was evidently caught up in a romantic image of Christmas from some bygone age which blinded him to the commercial realties of the season, which was just another opportunity (one of many) to drive consumer spending – that engine of economic growth for the spreading of comfort and prosperity, regardless of the cost to the planet. What could this man, this remnant of the past, know of such matters, for he was old and evidently not as mentality complete as a younger person? And what is wrong with commercialism in any case? This is good and proper and the way the world works; immutable and the only way that it can be – the one best way, as the material quality of life demonstrates! This at least is what Richard believed, as many do, but of course, this did not make him right, just very selective in that which he chose to accept as true! Pick the best and ignore all the bad aspects. No, that is not quite right. Please, dear reader, note my mistake, for what I really meant to say is, pick the best and convince yourself that the rest, those bad things, those inconvenient truths, they do not exist! This is the way of life, if you care to consider this, but perhaps you do not – too much of an inconvenient truth perhaps?

There is here a little bit of a mystery that may have escaped your attention, so I will point this matter out, and leave you to reflect on it while my story develops. What is this I am referring to? It was not something that Richard missed. How did the stranger know that Richard was a scientist? Very peculiar! More than peculiar, it was just plain weird, for this old man could not have known that Richard was a scientist. This was impossible. So how could it be?

This was an enigma; definitely one of those mysteries that science knows it can explain, or so scientific people think! An enigma it would, however, have to remain, for Richard, although wondering about the matter, was not prepared to ask the questions that he knew, or thought he knew, would lead to the explanation. Yes, he did want to know, to have the mystery resolved, but to discover this he would have to ask questions, and contrary to the image that the sciences would wish to portray, there are questions that scientists are not prepared to ask, for to do so would be to expose the feeble fundamentals on which science is constructed, and, as a corollary, the weak foundations upon which the western industrial world is built. To ask these questions would also mean engaging in more conversation. No, this would end here. No conversation. No discussion. No questions! Richard was adamant about this and had fully determined that he was not going to explore further. The sooner he was rid of this old man the better; this burden, this deadweight, this unwanted person who was holding him back from advancing towards his goal, to the party that awaited him. Very soon the opportunity to say goodbye would present itself to him. Only a short walk, a few more steps, until that moment arrived.

Before we move on to see that which happened next, I will say that it is a pity that he did not ask these questions, for he would surely have been surprised by the answers. This is part of the mystery of my story, so read on if you want to discover that which to I am referring.

Although it was Richard's intention to move as quickly as possible to the point where he could be rid of this burden, the old man had different ideas, for he was inclined to linger and began to reminisce about the sights he had seen over the years in this very agreeable display window, this place of magic and enchantment – that is, if you still are enchanted by your childhood; for the world, you should understand, has ways of making people feel disenchanted, not just with childhood, but with just about everything else as well.

"There are a countless number of different toys that I have seen in this window over the years," the old man informed Richard. "Today of course they are mostly electronic, but not so long back they were more traditional – dolls, constructor kits, painting and colouring implements, cars and trucks, dolls houses, and the like. Lots of plastic of course, as many modern artefacts are made from this material, even though it is a waste of the oil from which it is made; but who cares about such matters in a world obsessed with money and prosperity? But I can tell you," continued the stranger, "that there was an age when oil was not wasted in this way, for I can recall a period when just about all toys were made using wood or tin. In those now far off times, the choice of toys was much more limited than today – sometimes I wonder if the present generation is not going too far, and giving too much in the way of material items to their children and not enough of that which really matters."

"And what would that be?" asked Richard with a condescending tone, unable to hold back his question.

"Why do you need to ask?" responded the old man. "Surely it is self-evident."

Then there was silence as the old man waited for Richard to answer, but patently it was not as self-evident as the old man had indicated. Perhaps this is a strong indicator of that which is wrong with the modern world – that which should be obvious is not; too many important things now hidden in plain view? This is what it is to be blind! How comfortable!

"Um! It appears that the world has changed more than I suspected. It's love, young man. Love! That which, it seems, is fading from your world."

"Love! What do you mean love? This is something that happens to people. You know, man meets woman, they fall in love."

"It is one aspect of love, yes for sure. There are, however, many different types of love and you will find love at work in many different contexts. Love is why people help one another without expecting anything in return. Love is evident in many aspects of life, but not, I am afraid to say, in enough places to counter the greed, envy, and hatred that is consuming contemporary society. I think, young man, that you have a lot to learn about love."

"Yes, love can have its place, but certainly not in such matters as science and business," responded Richard.

"That, young man, is where you are wrong, and this will be your undoing as a species. Through stupidity you condemn yourselves, and the generations that follow, to living in a world dominated by ignorance and greed, where the strong prosper at the expense of the weak. You may well convince yourselves that this is the way of life, for humans are good at such self-deceptions, at hiding themselves from the truth. You have a phrase for it, don't you?"

"I don't know, do we?" Richard enquired, slightly curious to know what this could be.

The elderly stranger was quiet for a moment, gazing with those bright blue eyes, so full of life, into Richard's eyes, as though seeing right into his soul. Then the old man spoke the phrase that summarised mankind's collect delusions: "The emperor is wearing no clothes."

Richard had heard this many times before, but had never stopped to reflect on its real meaning. Suddenly, and for the first time in his life, he could see the deeper significance of the tale of the emperor's new clothes, as a fable of that which happens when people engage in collective denial and collective delusion.

"Why do you speak of such matters?" Richard asked.

"Because, young man, young scientist that you are, this is your tale, as it is for others of your inclination, such as engineers and technologists. Look around you. It's everywhere. You see people and organisations claiming to be thought leaders, but no sign can be seen of any leading thoughts; yet you participate in the delusion. People and organisations claim to be independent and unbiased, but they are not; yet you want to believe that they are. And the biggest delusion of all is that your world, your economic system, can be made to be sustainable, yet a profound analysis of the disparate issues and problems reveals that it is the very nature of the economic system, and of your science, engineering and technology, that are at the root of the problems. Yet still you persist in the collective delusion that sustainable economic development can be achieved if somehow a few minor adjustments can be made. About all these beliefs, only one thing needs to be said." Here the old man paused, and then delivered his final words on the matter. "The emperor, my young friend, is wearing no clothes!"

Why the conversation had moved on to such issues, and why this old man was able to talk in such a clear and profound way about these matters, Richard was unsure. He was also deeply troubled by the words just spoken. It was as though the foundations of his life had just been shaken, and that terrible feeling called doubt was starting to appear in his mind, stealthily beginning to destroy beliefs long held.

"It is time to move on," was all Richard was prepared to say to this, for now he was desperate to be rid of this fellow. There was no room in Richard's life for such thoughts and considerations, and he resented the old man who had dared to undermine the comfortable world that Richard had erected inside his head.

"You go," replied the old man, who now seemed, Richard thought, to want not to hold on to Richard's company any longer, as though he had in some mysterious way done that which he had intended. "I will stay here and observe these delightful toys a little while longer."

To Richard's great relief, the old man then let loose his grip on Richard's arm and, without a farewell, Richard moved off, instantly trying to put out of his mind what the old man had said; but he found this hard to accomplish, for the words spoken, few though they were, had left him feeling ill at ease with himself.

Crossing over to other side of the road, Richard glanced back over his shoulder. The old gentleman was still standing, gazing into the toy shop window, being also bathed in the warm yellow light that streamed forth from within. A few steps more and Richard branched from the main high street, up a side avenue; he looked back once more, but there was no sign of this stranger!

"Odd, where's he gone?" Richard asked himself, speaking aloud. "Ah well, who cares? He's not my problem."

These were words spoken to bring some comfort and reassurance back to that which had become a troubled mind, and to a degree this worked. And so it was that Richard went to his party and did that which people do at such events. He drank a little, ate some mince pies, talked with people about Christmas, the weather, and work, kissed a few people on the cheek, wished many, a merry Christmas.

Then he found himself back home, having not seen, on his return journey, any sign of the mysterious fellow whom he had encountered on his short walk between his home and his friend's house where the Christmas party was still taking place.

Richard sank into an armchair, having lit the log fire first, for it was a little chilly that evening in the house that Richard called home.

Soon the fire was ablaze, roasting his legs, and casting a dancing silhouette of flames on the wall opposite. This scene, one that is as old as man's relationship with fire, still stirs in the imagination images of times past, and, even in this modern age of gas and electric fires, offers a homely feel, even when there is not much that can be said to be homely. And what more of a Christmas image can one conjure up than a blazing fire? A scene completed by the many colourful Christmas cards that stood on all available surfaces, and, of course, the centrepiece of the decorations, this being a dark-green bushy Christmas tree standing in a corner of the room, all lit up with numerous coloured lights, some flashing, some not, and all reflecting and glinting in the many baubles that were attached to the branches of this lovely tree.

Then tiredness combined with the consequences of the alcohol intake at the party, and the soporific effect of the heat from the bright burning fire, took their toll and Richard slipped into a doze. But was it a restful slumber? Let us see!

How much time had passed by, Richard was unsure when, suddenly, he woke. The fire had died down, and a chill had once more begun to descend upon the room, but it was a chill the likes of which he had not previously known. This was not the effect of coldness with an earthly source, as might be expected on a winter's night. No, this was unearthly in origins, this chill, though not admitted as such by this man of the modern world, sitting as he was by the embers of a dying fire.

Richard fancied that there was a person seated in the chair opposite, watching him. Of course he knew that this was not so, for he lived alone and there were no guests, no visitors staying with him over the Christmas period. Yet he was watched!

"You're a figment of my imagination," he said aloud. Why he said this he was not sure, for he was not given to talking to people who were not present. But it was nevertheless reassuring to speak these words. No hero, you see, was Richard. There were, after all, things that frightened him, those shadows that lurk at the edge of light.

Yet, before his eyes there was … what exactly was it that was sitting there, watching him, and so very quietly? No denying this at all, there was someone there, for this registered in his brain. But no! Self-evidently a delusion of the mind brought on by tiredness, sleep, and alcohol. Just chemicals in the brain creating an image, neurones randomly firing, nothing real, only part of a chain of cause and effect leading to …. All explained! How nice not to have to resort to superstitious beliefs, to false notions. Science has the power to make all fully clear. And yet it watched him!

It watched him, and just sat there, oozing malice, yet it did not feel as such to Richard, for his brain was filled with good feelings. In his mind there were images of all the magnificent things that science, and the free-market economy which it now served, had done to add to the light of understanding, to increase material possessions and, yes, to spread comfort and prosperity. Two of man's greatest intellectual developments, science and industrial capitalism, now inexorably bound together, working to create a wonderful world and a splendid future. How perfect, how glorious, how enlightened, and how much it showed that there was no longer a need for God.

And while this awful creature watched Richard, they both in turn were watched.

Richard woke suddenly, leaving behind his dozing state. The fire was ablaze, as it had been only a few moments earlier when he had drifted off, beginning his slow decent into sleep. But something had agitated his mind, and brought him back to the surface of the world of the wakeful.

"Oh! It was a dream," he said, looking across towards the other chair, confirming that it was empty. "Just chemicals in the brain; neurons firing in a random manner! How spooky that was!"

Like many dreams it was bazaar, and, as with all dreams, it had the power to affect emotions, for Richard did feel a little strange and uneasy with himself, but not for long, for soon the heat of the fire was working its invisible magic once more, sending him into another one of those slumbers that come upon those ready for their bed, but who, for whatever reason, delay putting off the inevitable.

When he woke, the fire was still blazing, but more fiercely than it had initially, so evidently he had not slept for long. But sitting in the chair opposite was another creature, this time radiating peace and love. Yet another invention, Richard automatically assumed, of that peculiar, little understood and ephemeral thing we call the mind. Yet it watched him.

As with that darker being that had invaded Richard's brain, or as Richard thought, the creature that his brain had manufactured, this apparition, too, being this time one of the light, said nothing at all. It just gazed intensely at him, and filled his mind with much darker thoughts than the creature of the darkness had done. Not now did Richard perceive how good all was, and how man had created, or was in the process of creating, a paradise, one enabled by science, technology and the free-market enterprise; instead he saw the greed, the ignorance, and the arrogance of men whose minds were so fragmented by their disciplinary biases, dogmas, and vested interests that they were intellectually unable to see the problems that they were creating. Filling his mind were visions of war made more efficient by man's ingenuity, which not only enabled warfare more destructive than in any other age, but which also fuelled an economy where monsters cried out for the distrust and conflict that provided the jobs and the profits that kept the wheels of the economy turning and growing, spreading comfort and prosperity. What is more, the living planet was dying, as were the souls of men, and to crown this magnificent achievement, so-called men of God were powerless to stop this, and some even added to the destruction that was taking place everywhere.

As the creature of the light watched Richard, so it was that it also was watched, but not by the being of the darkness, for there was another entity also watching, and waiting!

Richard woke once more. The chair opposite was empty.

"Another dream! Must have eaten too much cheese," he said. "Everything can be explained! Strange night, though. First that mysterious old man, then these odd dreams that, I must admit, seem in a very peculiar way to be connected. And why does a dark creature fill my mind with pleasant thoughts, and a more angelic being create in my mind dark and unpleasant visions? That's the problem with dreams, they don't make much sense."

These oddities Richard pondered for a moment, specifically that a creature obviously connected to the darker side of human nature should engender thoughts that were warm and reassuring, while a vision plainly part of the goodness of humanity should convey images of darkness and destruction. "Perhaps these dreams are telling me something," he observed to himself at long last. "No; that's far too complex a thought for my mind! Better stick with cause and effect. There is no place for philosophy and spirituality in my world."

This for Richard was a reassuring thought – the complexity of the universe and of human existence reduced to a simplicity that his fragmented mind could cope with.

"Time for bed," Richard said, speaking aloud to himself. His, you see, was a lonely existence, where the world was explored and brought closer to a state of full understanding, but where his own inner self lay ignored, for it had no validity in a world that could only be understood in terms of theories, equations and experiments.

Thus, with the fire secured by a safety mesh that caged the flames in way that was analogous to how his mind was imprisoned by his beliefs, Richard retired to his bed, where he slept that untroubled sleep of one who has managed to silence the voice of the soul by finding fulfilment in the materialism of modern existence. But the soul cannot be silenced. Better listen to it!

Christmas day arrived, and for Richard it was much the same as any other day that he spent in this comfortable abode, this product of human endeavour that had taken men from hunters to explorers, from victims of circumstance to masters of their environment.

The morning passed, time relentlessly moving towards that appointed hour when he would, once more, set forth into the snow-covered world that lay beyond his door, taking yet more steps forward, undertaking one more short journey that would lead him on this occasion to another friend's house where he had been invited for Christmas Day lunch.

Thus, this journey he did make, although he walked through a village that was completely devoid of people, which even for Christmas Day was unusual, for there were always those who felt a need to stroll, regardless of weather, time of day, or season, as his encounter with that ageing man the night before had demonstrated. There was an unnatural atmosphere about the village that day but Richard, being a person of the modern world, was blind to this.

Soon he was knocking on the door of another comfortable home full of the fruits of modernity; that which masquerades as a meaningful life, when in truth, what hides behind this mask is naught but emptiness. Rat-a-tat-tat, rat-a-tat-tat. Twice he made this sound with his clenched fist, for the door bell was, he knew, broken; it had been so for years. Then he waited.

A few short moments passed and then the warm Christmas greetings, then a hug, and then the passing of coat, scarf and gloves to the host. Nigel was indeed in a good mood, full of Christmas cheer, for he was one who embraced the festive season, and, as one might say, celebrated Christmas well, as did his wife, Alison, who had now appeared in the hall. More hugs and Christmas greetings and a kiss.

"Come and meet Grandad," she said.

Alison led Richard into the lounge, where, sitting in an arm chair, close to the blazing coal fire, was an elderly gentleman whom Richard instantly recognised.

"We've already met," Richard informed Alison.

"Oh, how can that be? This is the first time Grandad has been here. He lives in a home. It's a long way away from here. We thought it would be nice for him to spend Christmas with family rather than being surrounded by carers and other elderly people."

"We met last night. In the village when your Grandad was out walking."

"What on earth are you talking about, Richard?" interjected Nigel. "He only arrived here this morning. I went to collect him. Must be someone else, or perhaps too much alcohol at that party. Or perhaps a ghost!"

Richard gazed at Alison's grandfather. There was no doubt about it – this was the person whom he had met the night before in the village. But Nigel and Alison were telling him that this could not be so, and they were not the sort of people to play a practical joke. If Nigel said that he had collected Alison's grandfather that morning from a home, many miles away, then he, Richard, had no reason to doubt it. The old man, however, looked at Richard with an expression on his face that said, "Oh yes, it was me all right!" But, of course, Richard knew that this was impossible!

Richard let the matter drop. Evidently he was mistaken, only he knew he was not. Then in due course, lunch, that highpoint of the Christmas Day celebration, appeared on the table. So they ate a hearty Christmas meal consisting of the traditional turkey, sprouts, chestnut stuffing, roast potatoes, cranberry sauce, carrots, and other items all crammed on a plate that under normal circumstances was big, but was not large enough for this seasonal feast. Thus it was that after this had been eaten, along with the Christmas pudding and brandy sauce, Nigel and Alison retreated to the kitchen to do tasks that must be done to reinstate order after such a banquet.

Richard was left alone with Alison's grandfather, each sitting in an armchair by the side of the glowing fire.

"So, have you thought about love yet?" asked the old man. Did your visitors last night teach you anything?"

Here was confirmation that Richard had not been mistaken. This old man, Alison's grandfather, was indeed the same person who, only the night before, Richard had encountered on the snow-covered street not too far from where they now sat.

"How is this possible?" Richard enquired. "This is ridiculous, unless some other person brought you here last night and then took you home again later."

"Ah, always looking for the logical explanation. Very modern! Very contemporary! But, how should I put this? Um! Ah yes, it was Shakespeare who wrote, 'There are more things in heaven and earth, Horatio, than are dreamt of in your philosophy.' I think this captures very well that which needs to be said. Very apt as well, given the nature of your philosophy, young scientist."

For a few seconds Richard was lost for words. He thought for a moment, and decided what he should say in response to this, but did not get the chance to speak, for the old man, carefully watching him, for he too watched, continued by saying, "Young scientist, I do not condemn science per se, just the way that you practise it in the modern world and your attitudes to other perspectives on the nature of humans and the universe. It doesn't have to be like this. There is choice, and if you have any common sense left inside that mind of yours, you will note my words, for you have already seen and been told by those creatures that visited you of the two sides to that which you do. You cannot continue with these simplistic beliefs any more. You need to change while you still have the chance. Time to walk a different path, and soon …"

~

"Wake up! Wake up! Richard! Wake up! You don't come to a party to sleep!"

These words, spoken in jest, reached into Richard's consciousness, raising awareness to the point where comprehension began to slowly drift into his mind, and then, after a few moments, he was awake, recognising his surroundings, recalling that he was at a Christmas Eve party, for as you will recall, dear reader, I did tell you that it was Christmas Eve, and to note this well for it is an important fact given that it is a time when strange events can happen. Now perhaps you understand a little more about why I stressed this point at the beginning of my story. But there is more to be said about this shortly.

"Sorry," responded Richard while slowly observing the scene before him, remembering that, having sat down to rest his tired legs, he had closed his eyes for a brief moment and then suddenly fallen into a deep sleep. "How long have I been asleep?" he enquired.

"Don't know," was the reply. "But you were talking in your sleep; something about angels and demons and other weird things. You were starting to scare people."

"Sorry," he said one more time. "I had a bad dream!"

"Sounded more like a nightmare! Get yourself a drink. Relax! Enjoy the Christmas festivities."

"Sure! Yes, I'll do that."

There was relief. It was only a dream! That explained much to Richard. Yet, coupled with the realisation that what had passed through Richard's mind, masquerading as reality, was but an invention, there still remained a residue of emotions that this knowledge did nothing to dispel. Deep within, there were images and words that rested uneasily with his beliefs, as though challenging him to change, to open his mind, to look beyond the details of the grains of sand that preoccupied his life, and to see the walls within which he had imprisoned himself. He had been invited to walk a different path.

Profound effects indeed for such a short period of time spent dealing with issues that otherwise never crossed his mind, in the Godless and soulless world of science in which he hid himself away. Such is the power of dreams!

But would it last or would he, within just a few hours, slip back once more into the quiet certainty that, in his world, God was nothing more than a delusion? Or would it be that he would open his eyes to greater truths that science, being still quite undeveloped and unsophisticated, was not able to explore?

An unexpected thought drifted into his perturbed mind and he found himself asking a most intriguing question. "Who exactly is deluded?" Evidently his mind had changed in some unknown way, which allowed what was once a cold logical thinking brain to reflect upon matters for which there can be no clear and definitive answer, at least not one that contemporary science is able to deliver. Was this the beginning of a journey without end, one without a final destination, where the mind does not close in on fixed opinions?

To ask who is deluded may be a sign that such a journey was beginning for the young scientist. It is certainly an important question. Is it those who believe in God who are deluded, or does the delusion reside in the minds of those atheists who argue that God is a delusion? Perhaps they are both deluded, for in reality it may be that one, not knowing the true nature of God but deludedly thinking they do, creates the material that the other uses to contemptuously argue the improbability of God's existence. The scientist, safe and secure in his impoverished world-view, reassured by the hubris of science, is unable to recognise the *bag of bones dressed up with a little good meat* that science currently is, and thus, being so constrained, cannot transcend what exists to create something worthy of the label *sophistication*.

The human mind, imprisoned by walled-in views, creates the hell within which people are condemned to live. Yet stepping out of this self-imposed intellectual cell is an option open to all, but few seem to want to make this journey, preferring instead the surety and comfort that comes with the familiarity of beliefs and ideologies. It is as though they are like a bird that has flown to a place where it does not want to be, but is too frightened to leave, even though the way out is clear. And this is one of the great tragedies of the human species. All should try to make the journey, for that which lies beyond their walled-in worlds will truly amaze them, and that applies to both scientist and priest.

'Tis Christmas Eve once more! See now, even more, why I stressed this point, for Christmas is a time for salvation, and who in this modern world are more in need of salvation than those caught up in collective delusions? Richard was beginning to open his eyes to this. Let us hope that he does not return to his old ways.

Richard's time at that Christmas social gathering was drawing to an end. He was no longer in a party mood. He quietly slipped away and walked the route back to his house, which of course took him past a certain toy shop window. As soon as he turned the corner he could see the old man standing just where he had left him, as though patiently waiting for Richard's return. So did Richard speak and behave differently towards this elderly gentleman? This I leave for you to conclude, for that which you choose as an ending will determine if there really is any hope left in this world.

The End